Let's Do That Again!

Hiawyn Oram

Illustrated by Sam Williams

DUTTON CHILDREN'S BOOKS ✦ NEW YORK

For Murray – S.W.

Text copyright © 2001 by Hiawyn Oram
Illustrations copyright © 2001 by Sam Williams
All rights reserved.

CIP Data is available.

Published in the United States 2003 by Dutton Children's Books,
a division of Penguin Putnam Books for Young Readers
345 Hudson Street, New York, New York 10014
www.penguinputnam.com

Originally published in Great Britain 2001 by Orchard Books, London
Typography by Gloria Cheng
Printed in Mexico • First American Edition
ISBN 0-525-46997-4
2 4 6 8 10 9 7 5 3 1

Mrs. Brownmouse and Little Brownmouse
were walking in the woods.
Mrs. Brownmouse hid behind a tree . . .

and popped out with a loud "BOO!"

Little Brownmouse jumped, and then she laughed and laughed. "Let's do that again!" she cried.

"Hmm, not now," said Mrs. Brownmouse,
"because right now it's time to go home."

So they turned around to go home, and just
when Mrs. Brownmouse wasn't expecting it . . .

Little Brownmouse hid
among the flowers . . .

and popped out with a loud "BOO!"

Mrs. Brownmouse jumped, and then she and Little Brownmouse laughed and laughed.

"Let's do *that* again!" cried Little Brownmouse.

"Hmm, not now," said Mrs. Brownmouse,
carrying Little Brownmouse high on her shoulders,
"because right now, it's time for dinner."

So they went home to make dinner, and Little
Brownmouse watched while Mrs. Brownmouse cooked.
And just when Mrs. Brownmouse wasn't expecting it . . .

Little Brownmouse crept
across the room and hid
behind the door . . .

and jumped out with a scary "AARGH!"

And Mrs. Brownmouse waved her wooden spoon
and growled "AARGH!" right back, which sent
Little Brownmouse running under the table, laughing
and laughing.

"Let's do *that* again!" she cried.

"Hmm, not now," said Mrs. Brownmouse, "because right now it's time to eat!"

So they sat down to eat, and Little Brownmouse played with her food and Mrs. Brownmouse ate her food . . .

and just as she was taking a rather
large mouthful, Little Brownmouse slid
down behind her chair . . .

then popped out with an eerie "WHO-O-O-O-O!"

Mrs. Brownmouse jumped up and ran after her,
crying, "What's a little ghost doing in my kitchen?"
And Little Brownmouse laughed and laughed.
"Let's do *that* again!" she cried.

"Hmm, not now," said Mrs. Brownmouse,
"because right now it's time for your bath."

So hand in hand, Mrs. Brownmouse
and Little Brownmouse went upstairs . . .

and Mrs. Brownmouse prepared Little Brownmouse's bath . . .

and Little Brownmouse got in.

Mrs. Brownmouse lathered up the sponge
and scrubbed Little Brownmouse all over. And just
when Mrs. Brownmouse wasn't expecting it . . .

Little Brownmouse made a big splash and soaked her!
Mrs. Brownmouse shrieked and splashed her right back,
and Little Brownmouse laughed and laughed.

Splash!

"Let's do *that* again!" she cried.

"Hmm, not now," said Mrs. Brownmouse, "because right now it's time for bed!"

So Mrs. Brownmouse toweled
Little Brownmouse dry . . .

and powdered her . . .

and tickled her toes.

Little Brownmouse
laughed . . .

and laughed . . .

Then Mrs.
Brownmouse
tickled her all
the way up . . .

from her chubby little toes . . .

to her furry little chin!

"Let's do *that* again!" Little Brownmouse cried. *"PLEASE!"*

"Hmm, not now," said Mrs. Brownmouse, "because right now it's time for your bedtime story."

So Little Brownmouse snuggled down under her blanket, and Mrs. Brownmouse read her a quiet bedtime story. And when it was finished . . .

Mrs. Brownmouse gave Little Brownmouse a hug,
and as Little Brownmouse hugged her back . . .

up the stairs crept
Mr. Brownmouse.

"Boo!" he cried.
Mrs. Brownmouse and
Little Brownmouse jumped,
then laughed and laughed.

"Shall we do *that* again?" said Mr.
Brownmouse.

"Oh, no! Not now!" cried Little
Brownmouse, "because right now it's
time for . . .

a great, big good-night hug!"